DATE DUE

⊏ ⊐ 3 '89   M 2

W9-AKE-188

j
M

12,018

Moncure, Jane Belk
    Just the right place. Illustrated by Helen
Endres.   Elgin, Ill., The Child's World, [1976]
    unp.   col.illus.

    1.Animals-Fiction.   I.Title.

EAU CLAIRE DISTRICT LIBRARY

Just the Right Place

EAU CLAIRE DISTRICT LIBRARY

written by *Jane Belk Moncure*

illustrated by Helen Endres

THE
CHILD'S
WORLD
ELGIN, ILLINOIS 60120

77487

Children's Press 11/19/76—@4⁹³

12,018

Distributed by Childrens Press, 1224 West Van Buren Street,
Chicago, Illinois 60607

Library of Congress Cataloging in Publication Data

Moncure, Jane Belk.
  Just the right place!

  SUMMARY: Because she can't turn anyone away, Ladybug
invites nine more animals to share her winter home.
  [1. Hibernation—Fiction. 2. Animals—Fiction]
I. Endres, Helen. II. Title.
PZ7.M739Ju   [E]   75-34176
ISBN 0-913778-36-2

© 1976 The Child's World, Inc.
All rights reserved. Printed in U.S.A.

One cold day, Ladybug went walking through the forest,
looking for a winter home.

"The geese have flown south,"
she said to herself as she hurried along.
"The leaves have fallen from the maple trees.
I must find a winter home before it snows."

Just then it began to snow.

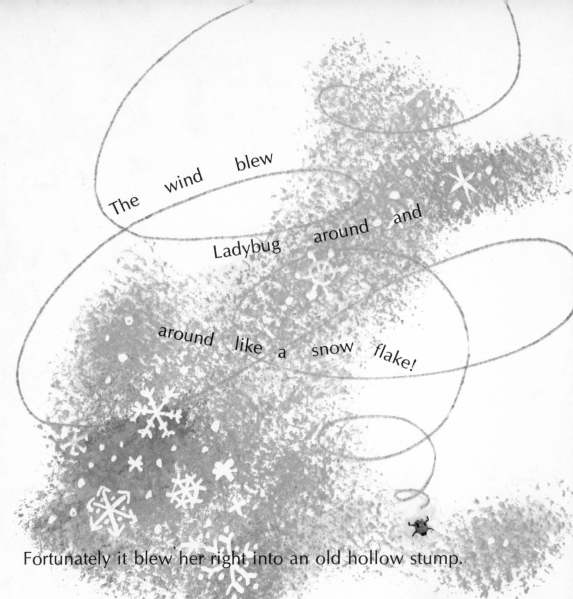

The wind blew Ladybug around and around like a snow flake!

Fortunately it blew her right into an old hollow stump.

The old stump was warm and dry inside.
Just the right place for a beetle to hide.
"No one lives here," said Ladybug. "I am all alone."
But suddenly there was a knock on the door.

There stood a little brown snail, shivering in the snow.

"Please, may I come in before I freeze?" asked Snail.

"Of course," said Ladybug. "There is room for you."

The old stump was warm and dry inside.
Just the right place for a snail to hide.
The two of them were about to settle down
when suddenly there was a knock on the door.

There stood a butterfly with her wings
wrapped around her like a coat.

"Please, may I come in before I freeze?"
asked Butterfly.

"Of course," said Ladybug. "There is room for you."

The old stump was warm and dry inside.
Just the right place for a butterfly to hide.
The three of them were about to settle down
when suddenly there was a knock on the door.

There stood a big, fat toad—hopping on one foot, then the other.

"Please let me in before I freeze!" he shouted.

Ladybug opened the door very slowly.
She knew toads like beetle meals.

"You may stay if you mind your manners," she said, trying to be polite.

"I promise," said Toad as he warmed his feet.

The four of them were about to settle down when suddenly there was a knock on the door.

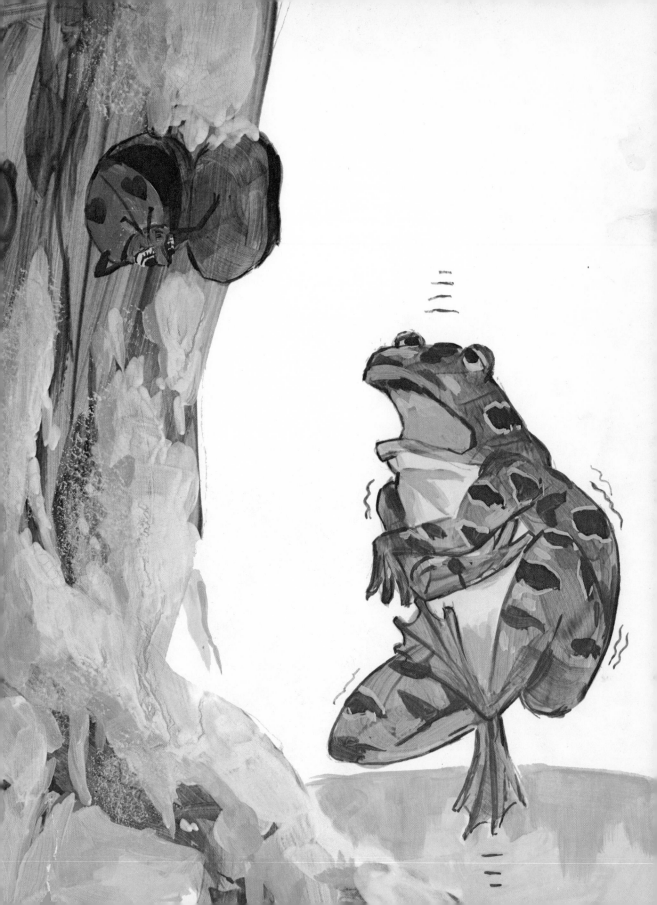

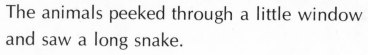

The animals peeked through a little window
and saw a long snake.

He looked like a green icicle.

"Please let me in before I freeze," he cried.

Toad opened the door very slowly.
He knew snakes like toad meals.

"You may stay if you mind your manners," Toad said,
trying to be polite.

"I promise," said Snake rather stiffly.

The five of them were about to settle down
when suddenly there was a knock on the door.

There stood a chubby little chipmunk.
She carried a basket of seeds and was dressed
in her warmest fur coat.

"I have lost my way," she said. "May I stay with you?"

"Of course," said Ladybug. "There is room for you."

The six of them were about to settle down,
when suddenly there was a knock on the door!

There stood a wood turtle.
His shell was covered with snow,
and he looked like a marshmallow cake.

"Please, may I come in before I freeze?" he asked.

"Of course," said Ladybug.

"It is getting crowded in here," said Toad grumpily.

"There is always room for a friend," said Butterfly.

The seven sleepy animals were about to settle down
when suddenly there was a knock on the door.

There stood Squirrel with an acorn in her paws.
"I have lost my way. May I stay with you?
I need a place to sleep."

"Of course," said Ladybug.
"The snow is getting so deep."

"Be careful where you step," said Toad grumpily.

Eight sleepy animals were about to settle down,
when suddenly there was a knock on the door.

There stood Skunk in her black and white fur coat.

"It is getting dark," she said. "May I stay with you
through the long winter night?"

"Well," began Ladybug, "we are a bit crowded."

"We can squeeze up a bit to make room for a friend,"
said Butterfly.

Toad was too sleepy to complain.
So Skunk squeezed inside the stump.

Nine sleepy animals were about to settle down
when suddenly there was a very loud knock on the door!

There stood Bear.
He was shaking the snow from his thick fur coat.

"May I come inside?" he asked in a huffy-gruffy voice.

"Of course, we will make room for you," said Ladybug.

The enormous bear was standing there.
What else could she do?

The stump was stuffed.

The ten animals agreed
that enough was enough!
So Ladybug made a little sign.

She hung it outside the door.
It read:
"No more room until spring!"

If you walk through the forest on a winter day
and see a stump—

                         tiptoe,
for you never know who might be sleeping there.